For David and his cottage, with love

First published in Great Britain 1985
by Methuen Children's Books Ltd
11 New Fetter Lane, London EC4P 4EE
Copyright © 1985 by Heather S Buchanan
Printed in Great Britain
by W. S. Cowell Ltd, Ipswich

ISBN 0 416 48560 X

# Matilda Mouse's First Adventure

Heather S. Buchanan

Methuen Children's Books

Matilda was a very small mouse. She lived with her parents in a beautiful teapot. The teapot had three cracks which met in a little triangular hole in its side, so it was no use for making tea any more.

Because the lid was also missing, it made an excellent home for the mouse family. No-one knew that they were inside it, and they came and went as they liked, only venturing out at night.

Matilda spent the early weeks of her life curled up in a mixture of sheep's wool and paper handkerchiefs, arranged to make a colourful nest at the bottom of the teapot.

In the few days before her eyes opened, she could reach her mother easily whenever she felt alone or thirsty. Later, when she had learnt to stand steadily, she began to crawl to the edges of the pot and peered up into the spout holes.

One night, Matilda's parents were out looking for stilton cheese and garibaldi biscuits.

Matilda moved all the sheep's wool to one wall, climbed on top of it, and stretched up on tiptoe until she could just reach the rim of the teapot. She gradually pulled herself up and out onto the edge, where she nearly overbalanced and learnt for the first time to use her tail to steady herself.

Matilda peered down into the kitchen
over the edge of the mantelpiece.
Suddenly, she felt very giddy and despite
her useful tail, a terrible thing happened –
she fell.

With her small body twisting and turning, her paws waving helplessly in the air, and her tail twitching, she somersaulted down and down.

She landed with a thud on something soft but firm. It was a patterned rug laid across the hearth.

Looking up, she saw the fire for the first time – a great furnace of heat and dancing flame. She felt the warmth on her little bruised body and was comforted by it while she waited for her heartbeats to grow calmer again.

Matilda looked carefully around her. As she stood only two inches from the ground on her toes, the cupboards and cooker looked to her like tall buildings.

She sniffed. There was a lovely scent of cheese somewhere and it drew her, whiskers twitching, towards the cupboard under the kitchen sink. Without further thought, she pulled herself up the door and eventually arrived at the sink top.

The piece of cheese was beside one of the taps and looked delicious. Matilda was very hungry now. Enthusiastically, she scampered past the tap but slithered on some soap.

The next minute she was floundering in
a washing-up bowl full of cold water and
soap suds. To her amazement, Matilda
Mouse discovered two things. She could
swim, and she was not alone.

A sponge was floating on the water and clinging to it, making a faint frightened noise, was a young ladybird. Its wings were getting wet because the sponge had filled with water and was growing heavier and sinking further all the time.

Matilda swam over and gently lifted the ladybird on to her head. She pushed her way through the bubbles until she reached the edge of the bowl. Climbing out was difficult but after several attempts they both sat safely on the draining board.

Matilda and the ladybird dried themselves together in the firelight. Then the ladybird said goodbye, thanked Matilda and set off to find its parents.

It ran to the edge of the draining board and tried to launch itself into the air. It fell over twice, but the third time it took off from its runway and whirred away into the shadows.

It was time for Matilda to go back home too. She ran to the edge of the sink, slid down the cupboard, scurried across the rug by the hearth and stopped at the fireguard. Using the black mesh of the guard as a ladder, she scampered up.

At the top was a line of horse brasses. She climbed from one to the next up to the mantelshelf, and squeezed into the safety of the teapot.

With great relief she wrapped herself in the sheep's wool and closed one eye. Her mother and father had not yet returned.

Hearing a little buzzing noise, Matilda looked up to see two flying ladybirds holding something, high above the teapot. As she stared, they let it drop on to the wool beside her.

It was a small, shining mother-of-pearl anchor with a little hole at the top – a charm from a bracelet.

'To thank you and bring you luck all your life,' the ladybirds called, and whirred away back into the ceiling shadows.

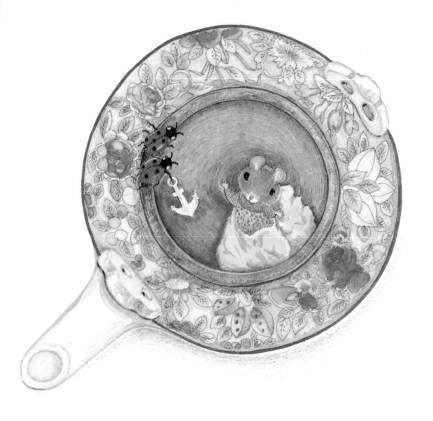

When Matilda's mother returned, she found her asleep, curled up in a ball with the anchor clasped tightly to her.

When Matilda woke up, her father made the anchor into a necklace for her with a piece of silk thread, while she told them all about how she rescued the ladybird.

The little anchor certainly did bring her luck, and she had many more adventures.